Most Intense College Football Rivalries

Kevin Yuen

Series Editor
Jeffrey D. Wilhelm

Much thought, debate, and research went into choosing and ranking the 10 items in each book in this series. We realize that everyone has his or her own opinion of what is most significant, revolutionary, amazing, deadly, and so on. As you read, you may agree with our choices, or you may be surprised — and that's the way it should be!

an imprint of

SCHOLASTIC

www.scholastic.com/librarypublishing

A Rubicon book published in association with Scholastic Inc.

 © 2008 Rubicon Publishing Inc.

www.rubiconpublishing.com

All rights reserved. No part of this publication may be reproduced, stored in a database or retrieval system, distributed, or transmitted in any form or by any means, electronic, mechanical, photocopying, recording, or otherwise, without the prior written permission of Rubicon Publishing Inc.

 is a trademark of The 10 Books

SCHOLASTIC and associated logos and designs are trademarks and/or registered trademarks of Scholastic Inc.

Associate Publishers: Kim Koh, Miriam Bardswich
Project Editor: Amy Land
Editor: Christine Boocock
Creative Director: Jennifer Drew
Project Manager/Designer: Jeanette MacLean
Graphic Designer: Jason Mitchell

The publisher gratefully acknowledges the following for permission to reprint copyrighted material in this book.

Every reasonable effort has been made to trace the owners of copyrighted material and to make due acknowledgment. Any errors or omissions drawn to our attention will be gladly rectified in future editions.

"The Play" (excerpt) permission courtesy of Joe Starkey — University of California football broadcaster.

Cover image: Notre Dame vs. USC–© Shelly Castellano/Icon SMI/Corbis

Library and Archives Canada Cataloguing in Publication

Yuen, Kevin
    The 10 most intense college football rivalries / Kevin Yuen.

ISBN 978-1-55448-545-1

    1. Readers (Elementary). 2. Readers — Football. I. Title.
II. Title: Ten most intense college football rivalries.

PE1117.Y84 2007   428.6   C2007-906858-8

Includes index.
ISBN: 978-1-55448-545-1

1 2 3 4 5 6 7 8 9 10   10   17 16 15 14 13 12 11 10 09 08

Printed in Singapore

Contents

Introduction: Turf Wars 4

Cal vs. Stanford 6
With a history that dates back to 1892, the Big Game has become the biggest college sporting event in the San Francisco Bay area.

Clemson vs. USC 10
Political and cultural clashes have set the stage for this bitter rivalry that began in 1909.

Harvard vs. Yale 14
Find out how the rivalry between two of America's most prestigious schools plays out.

Florida vs. Georgia 18
For one day a year, these two teams put their mutual "hate" aside and celebrate one of the most memorable events in college football.

Army vs. Navy 22
The Army-Navy game is a battle for national pride.

Florida State vs. Miami 26
Since 1983, these teams have won more national titles than any other two rivals in the country.

Oklahoma vs. Texas 30
Called the Red River Rivalry, this game brings together two teams with a long history of bitter feuds.

Alabama vs. Auburn 34
The annual game between the Crimson Tide and the Tigers is Alabama's version of the Super Bowl.

Michigan vs. Ohio State 38
These rivals feature some of football's brightest stars, playing in some of the most legendary games.

Southern California vs. Notre Dame 42
This rivalry is competitive and intense — and it has national appeal.

We Thought … 46

What Do You Think? 47

Index 48

TURF WARS

When you are playing sports, is there a person or team that you feel you must beat?

Whether it's baseball, basketball, or soccer, great rivalries exist in every sport. But few of them can match the longevity and passion of college football rivalries. These fiery match-ups have meant everything to generations of loyal fans. What's even more amazing is that college football rivals meet only once a year. The team that wins can claim bragging rights until the next big game. There is no prize money for the winning team. In some cases, there isn't even a trophy. But what is at stake is more important than material rewards — pride and dominance over long-standing rivals.

In this book, we present what we think are the 10 greatest rivalries in college football. In ranking them, we considered these criteria: What is the history of the rivalry? Does the rivalry involve long-standing traditions? Are there passionate fans and supporters? Are there memorable games? What is the national appeal of the rival teams?

It's often said that familiarity breeds contempt, and nothing illustrates this better than watching the teams on this list battle it out on the gridiron. Before you read on, think like a football expert and ask yourself:

---

contempt: *open disrespect*
gridiron: *football field*

10 CAL VS. STA[NFORD]

The University of California, Berkeley band marches on the field before a game at California Memorial Stadium.

USC

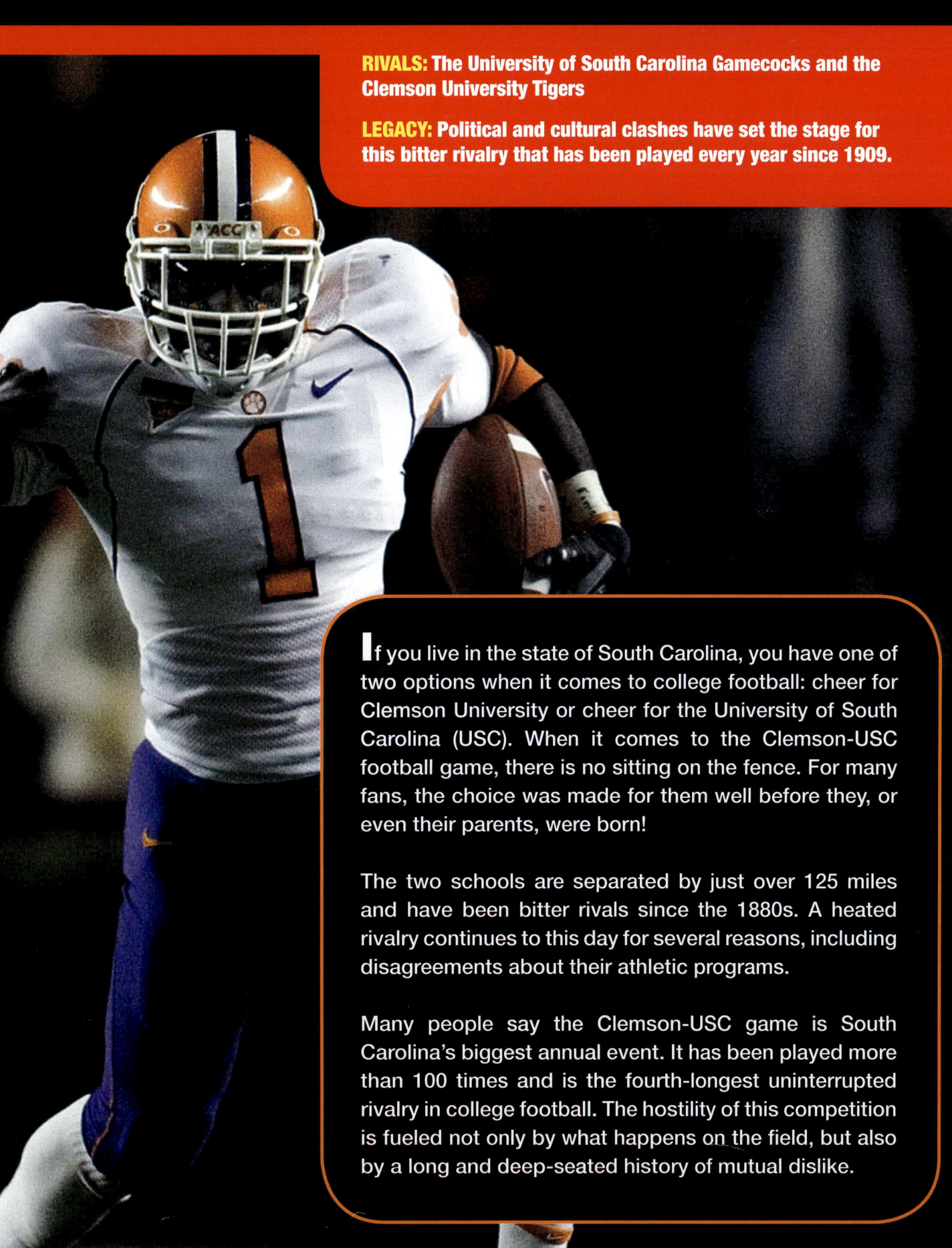

RIVALS: The University of South Carolina Gamecocks and the Clemson University Tigers

LEGACY: Political and cultural clashes have set the stage for this bitter rivalry that has been played every year since 1909.

If you live in the state of South Carolina, you have one of two options when it comes to college football: cheer for Clemson University or cheer for the University of South Carolina (USC). When it comes to the Clemson-USC football game, there is no sitting on the fence. For many fans, the choice was made for them well before they, or even their parents, were born!

The two schools are separated by just over 125 miles and have been bitter rivals since the 1880s. A heated rivalry continues to this day for several reasons, including disagreements about their athletic programs.

Many people say the Clemson-USC game is South Carolina's biggest annual event. It has been played more than 100 times and is the fourth-longest uninterrupted rivalry in college football. The hostility of this competition is fueled not only by what happens on the field, but also by a long and deep-seated history of mutual dislike.

CLEMSON VS. USC

HEAD TO HEAD

	CLEMSON	USC
Team's First Year	1896	1894
Home Stadium	Memorial Stadium	Williams-Brice Stadium
Mascot	Tiger	Cocky the Gamecock
Colors	Orange and Maroon	Garnet and Black

George Rogers is awarded the Heisman Trophy in 1980.

Quick Fact
The Heisman Trophy is named after John Heisman, a college football star who coached the Clemson team for four seasons. The trophy is awarded every year to the most outstanding college football player in the United States.

KICKOFF
This rivalry started long before the first game was ever played! The founders of Clemson University felt that the state's main university, the University of South Carolina, only focused on grooming doctors and lawyers and did not give enough help to farmers. As such, Clemson University was established in 1889 to stand for everything that USC did not. The first football game between the rivals was played in 1896. Due to serious tensions between the schools, the game was suspended between 1902 and 1909. Since 1909, Clemson and USC have faced off annually in what is now known as the "Battle of the Palmetto State."

palmetto: *referring to any of various palms having fan-shaped leaves*

STAR PLAYERS
Clemson: William "The Refrigerator" Perry is the most recognizable player to come from Clemson's football program. He was a good player in college, but gained worldwide popularity playing with the NFL's Chicago Bears. Perry was known for his gigantic size and was an immovable force on the field — he stood at 6'2" and weighed close to 350 pounds.

USC: As USC's starting running back, George Rogers set many Gamecock records. He was the most celebrated running back in the school's history and many of his records still stand today. Rogers was awarded the Heisman Trophy in his senior year. The New Orleans Saints made him the first overall pick of the 1981 NFL draft.

running back: *offensive player who runs with the football*

The Expert Says…
"There's a history of bad blood between these institutions. … The rivalry extends back to political and social origins. It's not just an athletic rivalry. It's a manifestation of these things."

— Jay McCormick, doctoral candidate, University of South Carolina

manifestation: *expression*

? How do you think sports rivalries are intensified when political and social differences are involved?

A Clemson quarterback drops back to pass.

A RIVALRY IN THE MAKING

This intense in-state rivalry is remembered for several infamous events. Read about its history in the **fact cards** below.

1902: BRAWL #1
One day before the game, USC fans showed up with posters of a gamecock standing on top of a tiger. USC ended up beating the highly favored Clemson. After the game, Clemson fans warned USC fans about waving the posters at the post-game parade. USC fans ignored their warnings and a full-scale fight broke out.

1946: TICKETGATE
Counterfeiters tried to profit from the game's popularity by selling fake tickets. Once the stadium had been filled, fans with both real and fake tickets were denied entry. As the angry mob grew larger, organizers allowed them to watch from the sidelines. U.S. Secretary of State James Byrnes had to step in to calm down the rowdy crowd.

1961: THE PRANK
Before the game, members of a USC fraternity dressed up like Clemson players and performed warmups on the field. The Clemson band thought they were actually Clemson players and started playing the school's theme song. Meanwhile, the fake Clemson players acted silly in front of the crowd. When Clemson fans figured out they were imposters, many became angry. Security stepped in before the situation got out of hand.

2004: BRAWL #2
After a lopsided loss in 2003, USC still had hard feelings as they headed into 2004's game. In the fourth quarter a Clemson player punched the USC quarterback. Chaos followed and state troopers were called in to break up the fight.

fraternity: *social order for men at a university*

Quick Fact
Twelve players were suspended after the 2004 brawl, six from each school. In a move to improve sportsmanship, a pre-game handshake was added before the 2005 game.

? The rivalry between Clemson and USC has gotten out-of-hand at times. Why do you think players and fans can get so worked up over a game?

Take Note
The Clemson-USC rivalry is not just about football. Passionate fans, historic tensions, and mutual dislike place this rivalry at #9 on our list. And because South Carolina does not have a professional football team, the state's football fans focus on Clemson and USC.
- Compare this rivalry with the Cal-Stanford rivalry at #10. What is similar or different?

8 HARVARD VS.

The Harvard Crimson and the Yale Bulldogs in action, November 21, 1998

YALE

RIVALS: The Harvard University Crimson and the Yale University Bulldogs

LEGACY: This is one of the first college football rivalries in the United States.

The rivalry between Harvard and Yale is known simply as "The Game." Involving two of America's oldest and most famous schools, this rivalry is surrounded by history and long-standing traditions.

Being part of the Ivy League, Harvard and Yale athletes do not receive sports scholarships. Ninety-nine percent of the athletes play without a chance of making the NFL. They play simply for the sake of competition and love of football.

The Harvard-Yale game takes place at the end of each team's regular season. For graduating players, this makes "The Game" even more meaningful. It is the final game of the season. For most, it is also the final game of their football careers.

With so many famous and powerful alumni from each school, the impact of the Harvard-Yale rivalry is felt far beyond the Cambridge and New Haven campuses.

Ivy League: *alliance of eight universities in the Northeast; each school has a reputation for academic excellence*
campuses: *the grounds, including the buildings, of colleges and universities*

HARVARD VS. YALE

HEAD TO HEAD

	HARVARD	YALE
Team's First Year	1874	1875
Home Stadium	Harvard Stadium	Yale Bowl
Mascot	John Harvard (Pilgrim figure)	Handsome Dan (the Bulldog)
Colors	Crimson	Yale Blue

KICKOFF

The Harvard-Yale rivalry has great historical importance. The Game was first played in 1875. Since then, the teams have met 123 times. The rivalry has led to the creation of many game-day traditions, such as fight songs and mascots. Because the first contests in this rivalry were some of the first football games ever played, many rules that were made up at these games became part of the official rulebook. One of these was to replace goals with touchdowns to decide a game. Another was to replace the round rubber ball with the egg-shaped leather ball.

STAR PLAYERS

Harvard: Freshman Isaiah Kacyvenski won Ivy League Rookie of the Year. He graduated as Harvard's all-time leading tackler. In 2000, he was drafted in the fourth round by the NFL's Seattle Seahawks. This is the highest draft position ever for a Crimson player.

Yale: Larry Kelley and Clint Frank won the second and the third Heisman Trophies ever awarded. Kelley won his trophy in 1935, and Frank in 1936. They are the only two Ivy League players to have ever won the Heisman Trophy. Kelley was inducted into the College Football Hall of Fame in 1969.

tackler: player who wrestles the opposing ballcarrier to the ground, ending the play

Quick Fact

The 1968 Harvard-Yale game is considered one of their greatest. Yale had won 16 games in a row. Harvard had a terrible 0–8 record for the season. Trailing 29–13 with less than a minute to go, Harvard scored a touchdown, made the two-point conversion, recovered the onside kick, scored again on the game's final play, and made another two-point conversion to tie the score at 29. The next day the headline of the Harvard school paper read, "Harvard beats Yale 29–29."

two-point conversion: on the play after a touchdown, an attempt to reach the end zone for two points, instead of a kick for one point
onside kick: attempt by the kicking team to recover the ball after kicking it a short distance

Bulldog Handsome Dan

The Expert Says…

"The Game is the highlight of the football season for both teams and for their fans. The excitement of the competition is intense and unforgettable with fight songs ringing in the crisp autumn air."

— Alan Bersin, Harvard alumnus and former offensive guard from 1964–1967

THE PRANK

The Harvard-Yale rivalry reached its peak when Yale students played a world-class prank on unsuspecting Harvard. This **account** explains how it went down.

Archrivals on the field

SCENE: "The Game"
WHERE: Harvard Stadium
WHEN: 2004
PRANKSTERS: Yale students Michael Kai and David Aulicino

TALE: Kai and Aulicino dressed up in "Harvard Pep Squad" shirts and painted their faces red. Along with 20 other Yale imposters, the "Harvard Pep Squad" (which doesn't really exist) began handing out red and white cards to Harvard fans. They told fans the cards would make up a "Go Harvard!" message when raised all at the same time. They got the unsuspecting Crimson fans to raise their cards in the first and second quarters. To everyone's surprise, the 1,800 cards actually spelled out an obscene expression, much to the delight of Yale supporters and embarrassment of Harvard fans.

At the time, Harvard students, teachers, and alumni who held up the cards didn't even realize what had happened. When asked, Aulicino admitted, "We pulled it off too well." It wasn't until later when the Yale students posted the prank online that the Crimson supporters knew what had hit them.

Quick Fact

One of the most famous people to ever attend Harvard University dropped out before graduating. After his sophomore year, Bill Gates left Harvard to focus on his software company called Microsoft. Gates's success with Microsoft has made him one of the wealthiest people in the world.

? Harvard and Yale actually helped to develop the sport of football in the United States. How do you think this adds to the greatness of their rivalry?

? Students at both Harvard and Yale have played many good-natured pranks on each other over the years. Do you think pranks raise or lower school spirit? Explain.

Take Note

The Harvard-Yale rivalry scoops up the #8 spot on our list. This rivalry goes all the way back to 1875 and helped to invent the sport of football. It has a broad fan base of passionate supporters that includes famous and powerful alumni.
- Harvard and Yale do not award athletic scholarships. Why is this rivalry so popular, despite not having NFL-quality players?

5 4 3 2 1

7 FLORIDA VS.

Wide receiver Percy Harvin of the Florida Gators is tackled by Reshad Jones of the Georgia Bulldogs on October 27, 2007.

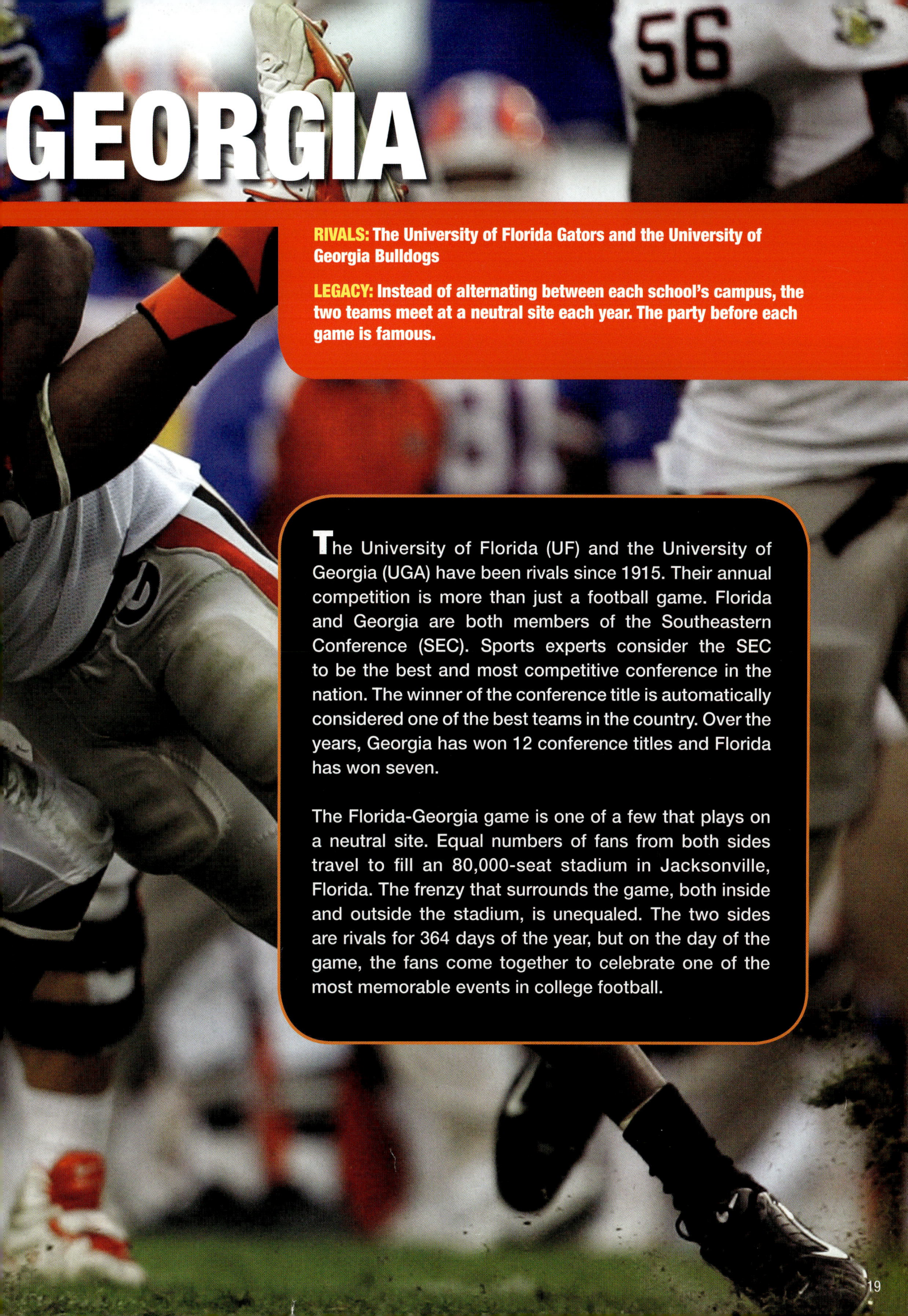

GEORGIA

RIVALS: The University of Florida Gators and the University of Georgia Bulldogs

LEGACY: Instead of alternating between each school's campus, the two teams meet at a neutral site each year. The party before each game is famous.

The University of Florida (UF) and the University of Georgia (UGA) have been rivals since 1915. Their annual competition is more than just a football game. Florida and Georgia are both members of the Southeastern Conference (SEC). Sports experts consider the SEC to be the best and most competitive conference in the nation. The winner of the conference title is automatically considered one of the best teams in the country. Over the years, Georgia has won 12 conference titles and Florida has won seven.

The Florida-Georgia game is one of a few that plays on a neutral site. Equal numbers of fans from both sides travel to fill an 80,000-seat stadium in Jacksonville, Florida. The frenzy that surrounds the game, both inside and outside the stadium, is unequaled. The two sides are rivals for 364 days of the year, but on the day of the game, the fans come together to celebrate one of the most memorable events in college football.

FLORIDA VS. GEORGIA

HEAD TO HEAD

	FLORIDA	GEORGIA
Team's First Year	1906	1892
Home Stadium	Ben Hill Griffin Stadium	Sanford Stadium
Mascot	Albert E. Gator	Uga VI (the Bulldog)
Colors	Orange and Royal Blue	Red and Black

Quick Fact

The Florida-Georgia game takes place at Jacksonville Municipal Stadium, which is a neutral site for both schools. The two schools split the tickets equally. Outside the stadium, another 30,000 fans add to the festive party atmosphere.

KICKOFF

These competitors can't even agree on when their rivalry began. According to the Bulldogs, they first played (and beat) the Gators in 1904. The Bulldogs count this game as a win in their record books. But the University of Florida wasn't founded until 1905, and their football team didn't officially exist until 1906. According to Florida, their first game in the series was in 1915, when they lost in a 39–0 blowout.

STAR PLAYERS

Florida: Steve Spurrier was the quarterback for the Florida Gators in the 1960s. He received a Heisman Trophy in 1966. After retiring from the NFL, he went on to great fame as Florida's head football coach from 1990–2001. During those 12 seasons, the Gators finished in the top 10 nine times and won the school's first national title.

Georgia: Herschel Walker is considered one of the greatest college football players ever. His advantage was his incredible physical fitness. He won the Heisman Trophy in 1982 and went pro in 1983. He retired in 1997 as one of the NFL's top ballcarriers, gaining more yards than any other player in professional football history.

 Do you think the 1904 game should count in the record books? Why or why not?

The Expert Says...

"[T]he Florida-Georgia game is truly one of the great rivalries in college football. The thing that separates this one is the fact that it's played at a neutral site."

— Urban Meyer, University of Florida head coach (2005–present)

Florida's marching band on the field before a game at the Ben Hill Griffin Stadium

CLASSIC GAME

THIS ARTICLE DETAILS THE RIVALRY'S MOST FAMOUS GAME.

In 1980, Georgia headed to Jacksonville for its annual game with Florida in the middle of its best-ever season. Even though the Bulldogs weren't a preseason favorite, they had won their first eight games thanks to the brilliance of their running back Herschel Walker. One more win and Georgia would earn a chance to play for the national title.

The Florida Gators were eager to dash the dreams of their favored rivals. With little more than one minute left in the game, the Gators had the Bulldogs right where they wanted them. Florida held a 21–20 lead and had Georgia pinned on their own seven-yard line. Needing to gain eight yards to make the game last a few more seconds, the Bulldogs completed a miracle pass play. Georgia quarterback Buck Bellue tossed the ball to Lindsay Scott, who avoided all would-be tacklers and sprinted 93 yards to score the game-winning touchdown.

The 1980 game is often remembered as the greatest contest in this rivalry. The undefeated Georgia Bulldogs went on to win the Sugar Bowl and earn their first (and only) national championship.

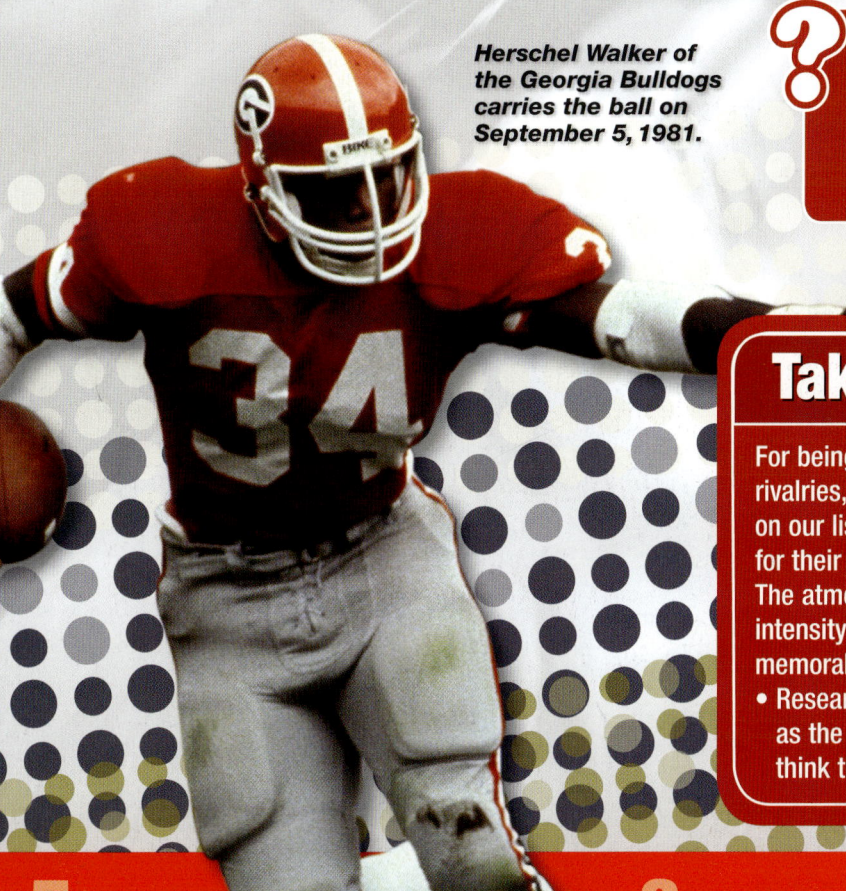

Herschel Walker of the Georgia Bulldogs carries the ball on September 5, 1981.

? Would you rather lose to a fierce rival by a wide margin or in a close game? Think of another game you have watched or played that wasn't decided until the very end. How did it make you feel?

Take Note

For being one of the most competitive college football rivalries, the Florida-Georgia teams take the #7 spot on our list. Their fans and supporters are well known for their competitive spirit and passionate loyalties. The atmosphere around the games adds to the intensity of the rivalry and makes it one of the most memorable in college football.
- Research some of the traditions of this rivalry, such as the mascots and the fight songs. How do you think they add to the rivalry between the two teams?

6 ARMY VS. NA

Cornerback Bas Williams (#6) of the Navy Midshipmen tries to tackle fullback Craig Stucker (#36) of the Army Black Knights.

RIVALS: United States Military Academy (Army) Black Knights and the United States Naval Academy (Navy) Midshipmen

LEGACY: This rivalry is probably the most tradition-filled of any sport.

This game was once played with the national title in mind. But lately, neither school boasts influential football programs or attracts the nation's top high-school athletes. And the teams rarely come into this game with winning records. So why is the Army-Navy rivalry so great?

Like the Harvard-Yale rivalry, the Army-Navy game is played for the love of football. The pure competitive spirit is what keeps this rivalry popular. Even though there are no hopes for a national championship, the Army-Navy game is a battle for national pride. It's the most exciting game of the year for the cadets of both schools.

The Army-Navy rivalry is full of honored traditions. Both sides are known for their sportsmanship. Regardless of who wins, all players and fans stand at the end of each game to honor their alma maters. It is a show of respect for the schools that produce these outstanding athletes.

cadets: *students who are in school to become officers in the military*
alma maters: *originally a Latin phrase, it refers to schools or colleges that individuals have attended*

ARMY VS. NAVY

HEAD TO HEAD

	ARMY	NAVY
Team's First Year	1890	1879
Home Stadium	Michie Stadium	Navy-Marine Corps Memorial Stadium
Mascot	Mule	Bill the Goat
Colors	Black and Gold	Blue and Gold

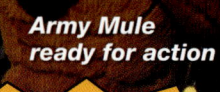

Army Mule ready for action

Quick Fact
The Navy weight room features weight plates that are stamped with the slogan "Beat Army."

KICKOFF

The first Army-Navy game was played in 1890. Navy routed Army by a score of 24–0! In 1893, Navy won a bloody 6–4 victory over Army. After fights broke out in the stands, President Grover Cleveland banned the Army-Navy game. It was restarted in 1899 after Teddy Roosevelt, then Secretary of the Navy and future president, sent a letter to the Secretary of War. Since then, the game has been played over 100 times.

STAR PLAYERS

Army: Doc Blanchard and Glen Woodward Davis formed a fearsome running pair in the mid-1940s. They set a record with 97 combined touchdowns, which stood for nearly 60 years. Blanchard won the Heisman Trophy in 1945 and Davis won it in 1946.

Navy: Roger Staubach won the Heisman Trophy in 1963 while quarterbacking the Midshipmen to the second-best ranking in college football. He served five years of military service, including a one-year tour to Vietnam during the war. He went on to great success in the NFL. Stauback led the Dallas Cowboys to two Super Bowl victories, and was inducted into the Pro Football Hall of Fame in 1985.

The Expert Says...

" [I]t is played by teams who try to crush each other for three hours, then stand at attention together when the game is over. "

— John Feinstein, author of *A Civil War: Army vs. Navy*

Navy quarterback Roger Staubach looks to pass the ball.

COMMANDER-IN-CHIEF'S TROPHY

This **article** explains why this prize is more than just a regular trophy.

The Commander-in-Chief's Trophy is awarded to each season's winner of the triangular college football series among the U.S. Army, Navy, and Air Force. It is the only college football trophy that involves more than two teams. The Navy-Air Force game is played in October, the Army-Air Force game in November, and the Army-Navy game in December. If there is a tie, the award is shared. The trophy was first awarded in 1972 and is named for the President of the United States, who acts as Commander-in-Chief of all U.S. military services.

The trophy was meant to give special meaning to games played among the U.S. Army, Navy, and Air Force. Unlike other college football rivalries, these teams know that the players they are competing against are soldiers, pilots, and marines who will serve beside them after graduation.

Quick Fact
At the end of every game, the fight songs of the losing team and then the winning team are played. The winning team stands alongside the losing team and faces the losing academy's students. Then the losing team turns and salutes the fans of the victors. This is a tradition to show respect and unity.

Navy Midshipmen Luke Penrose (left) and Marco Nelson (right) raise the Commander-in-Chief's Trophy after defeating the Black Knights on December 3, 2005.

? Do you think such a unique trophy sets this rivalry apart from the college football rivalries you have read about so far? Explain.

Take Note
The Army-Navy rivalry takes the #6 spot. The sportsmanship, honor, and respect displayed by the competing teams make it one of the most memorable rivalries on our list. The 1942 game was a great example. It took place during World War II, and traveling to the game was difficult for Army supporters. The Navy ordered some of their midshipmen to sit with the visiting Army supporters to help cheer for the Army team.
- Does this show of sportsmanship affect how you would rank the Army-Navy rivalry? Why or why not?

? Why do you think Army and Navy players display such respect for each other after each game?

5 FLORIDA STATE

This rivalry may not be one of the oldest on our list, but it is definitely one of the most intense. Between 1983 and 2002, the rivalry between Florida State University (FSU) and the University of Miami was considered the biggest and the best. Thirteen out of those 20 years, both teams entered the game with a top-ten ranking. At least one of these teams was ranked in the top six during those years. Since 1983, Florida State and Miami have combined to win seven national titles — more than any other pair of rivals in the country.

At their peak, Florida State and Miami dominated college football because they were able to recruit the best high-school players to their programs. Hundreds of these players have gone on to the NFL. Thanks to all this talent, Florida State and Miami have competed in some of college football's greatest and most intense games. Because a number of the most memorable games were settled by a single kick that went wide of the goal posts, the term "wide right" will always be associated with the FSU-Miami rivalry.

VS. MIAMI

RIVALS: The Florida State University Seminoles and the University of Miami Hurricanes

LEGACY: Since 1983, these teams have won more national titles than any other two rivals in the country.

Wide receiver Chris Davis of the Florida State Seminoles (#5) has a pass knocked away by defensive back Kelly Jennings of the Miami Hurricanes (#22).

FLORIDA STATE VS. MIAMI

HEAD TO HEAD

	FLORIDA STATE	MIAMI
Team's First Year	1947	1926
Home Stadium	Doak Campbell Stadium	Miami Orange Bowl
Mascot	Chief Osceola	Sebastian the Ibis
Colors	Garnet and Gold	Orange and Green

Quick Fact
In 1947, Florida State chose the name "Seminoles" to honor the local Seminole tribe. The Seminoles are a courageous and determined people who have struggled to preserve their culture and live according to their own traditions. The school has worked hard to make sure they represent the Seminole tribe with respect.

KICKOFF
Florida State and Miami first faced off in 1951, but didn't start playing every year until 1966. This became the best college football rivalry during the 1980s and 1990s. Between 1983 and 2002, the Hurricanes and Seminoles won a total of seven national championships between the two (five for Miami, two for FSU) and played in a total of 14 national championship games.

STAR PLAYERS
Florida State: Deion Sanders (aka Prime Time) is one of the most famous athletes to ever come out of FSU. He was a three-sport star in football, baseball, and track. After college he played both professional football and baseball. On the football field, he is widely recognized as one of the greatest cornerbacks in the history of college and professional football.

> Deion Sanders is not the only athlete in this book who has played more than one sport. How do you think playing multiple sports can improve an athlete's performance?

Miami: Bernie Kosar helped lead Miami's football program to national fame in the early 1980s. Playing quarterback, he put the Hurricanes on the map by leading the team to its first ever national title. After college, Kosar had a long and successful career in the NFL. He played most of his pro career with his hometown team, the Cleveland Browns.

cornerbacks: *defensive players whose primary purpose is to defend against the pass*

Miami Hurricanes quarterback Bernie Kosar looks for an open receiver.

The Expert Says...
"Both teams know the story. This game, you better be ready to play."
— Bobby Bowden, head coach of Florida State Seminoles

Just for Kicks

On more than one occasion, the Florida State Seminoles have lost to their Miami Hurricane rivals because of missed field goals. This report describes FSU's heartbreaking defeats.

WIDE RIGHT I: In 1991, the Hurricanes traveled to Tallahassee to face the Seminoles. Miami had a 17–16 lead in the fourth quarter, but they left enough time for FSU to set up a game-winning field goal attempt. FSU kicker Gerry Thomas had already made three kicks that day. Everyone watching thought it was a sure thing. When the kick sailed "wide right," a curse was born.

WIDE RIGHT II: In 1992, the Seminoles were determined to avenge the previous year's heartbreaking loss. Miami was trailing at the start of the fourth quarter, but they scored nine straight points to take a 19–16 lead. Like the previous year, FSU drove down the field to set up a last-second field goal. History repeated itself when kicker Dan Mowery pushed the 39-yard kick wide right. It cost FSU a chance at a national title. Miami went on to lose in the national championship game to the University of Alabama.

WIDE RIGHT III: In 2000, #7 Miami hosted top-ranked Florida State. With 46 seconds left, the Hurricanes took a 27–24 lead with a classic length-of-the-field touchdown drive. But the game was not over. Quarterback Chris Weinke drove the Seminoles into field goal range. This gave Matt Munyon a chance to kick a long field goal and tie the game. Miami escaped with the win as the kick sailed wide right.

WIDE LEFT: In 2002, the #1 Hurricanes were clinging to a 28–27 lead with just a few minutes remaining in the game. FSU once again had a last-second chance to get over their kicking curse. But again they failed. This time, kicker Xavier Beitia's 43-yard kick sailed wide left.

drive: *series of plays that begins when an offense takes the ball and lasts until it scores or turns the ball over to the other team*

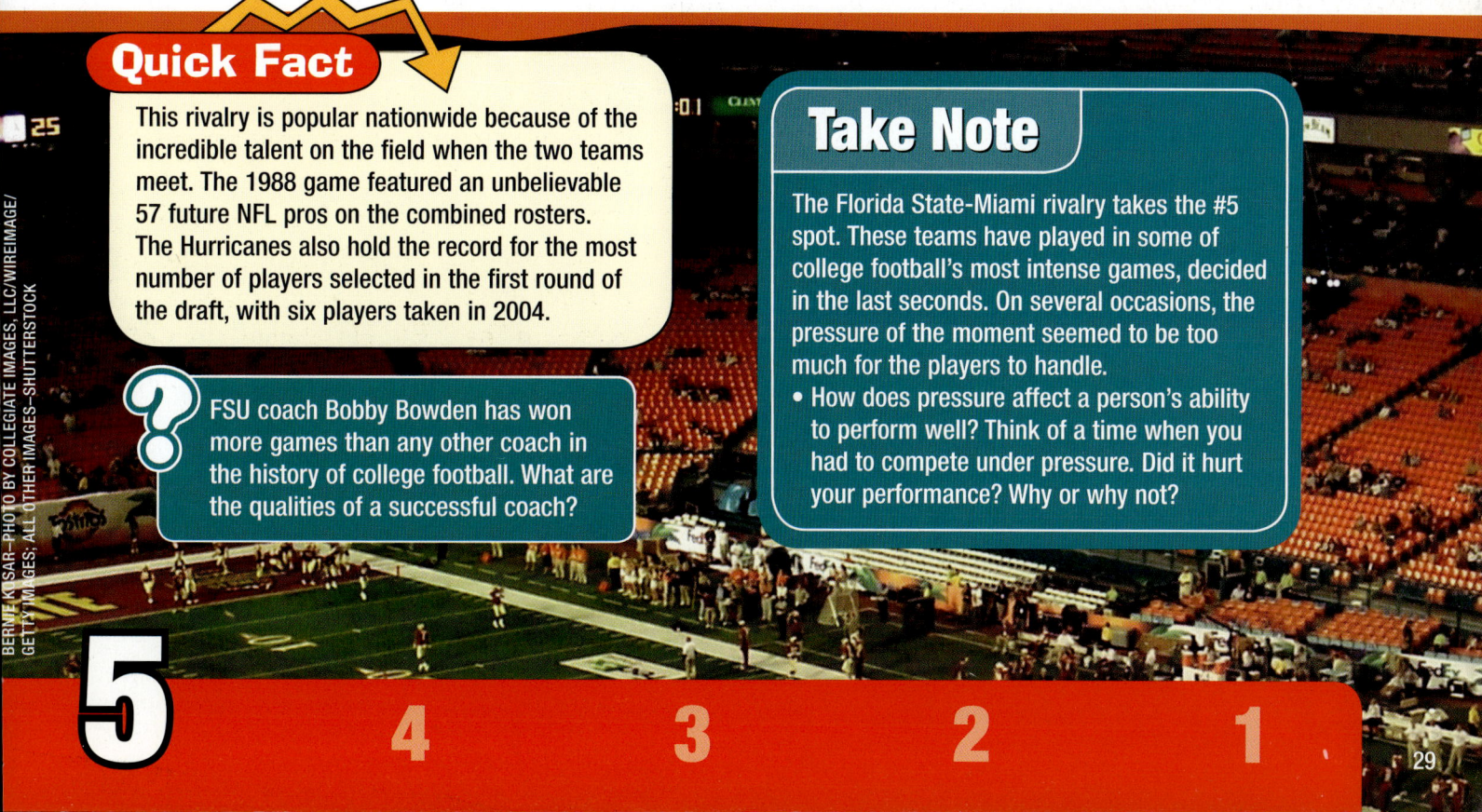

Quick Fact
This rivalry is popular nationwide because of the incredible talent on the field when the two teams meet. The 1988 game featured an unbelievable 57 future NFL pros on the combined rosters. The Hurricanes also hold the record for the most number of players selected in the first round of the draft, with six players taken in 2004.

? FSU coach Bobby Bowden has won more games than any other coach in the history of college football. What are the qualities of a successful coach?

Take Note
The Florida State-Miami rivalry takes the #5 spot. These teams have played in some of college football's most intense games, decided in the last seconds. On several occasions, the pressure of the moment seemed to be too much for the players to handle.
- How does pressure affect a person's ability to perform well? Think of a time when you had to compete under pressure. Did it hurt your performance? Why or why not?

5   4   3   2   1

④ OKLAHOMA VS.

Tight end Jermichael Finley of the Texas Longhorns scores a touchdown against the Oklahoma Sooners.

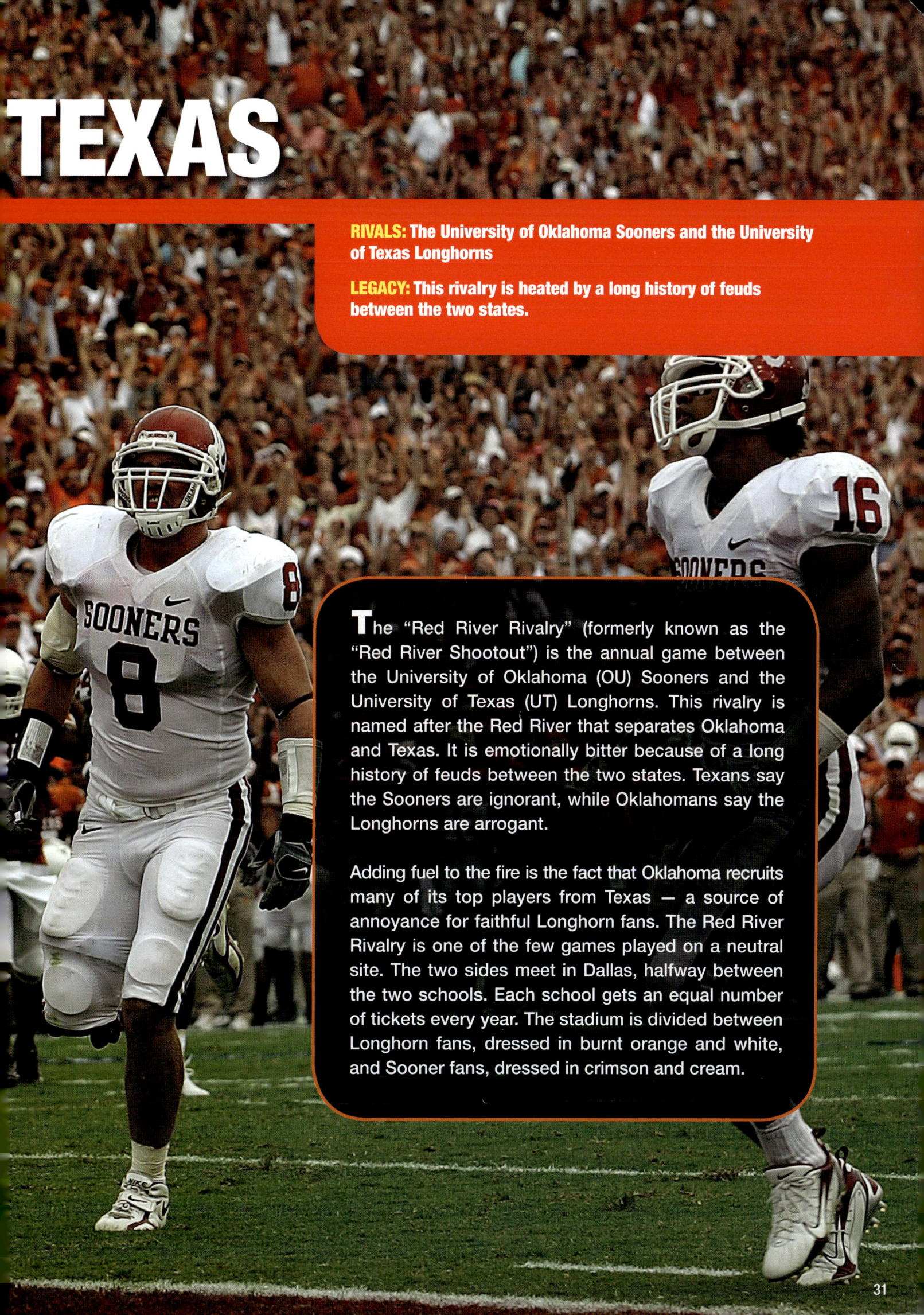

TEXAS

RIVALS: The University of Oklahoma Sooners and the University of Texas Longhorns

LEGACY: This rivalry is heated by a long history of feuds between the two states.

The "Red River Rivalry" (formerly known as the "Red River Shootout") is the annual game between the University of Oklahoma (OU) Sooners and the University of Texas (UT) Longhorns. This rivalry is named after the Red River that separates Oklahoma and Texas. It is emotionally bitter because of a long history of feuds between the two states. Texans say the Sooners are ignorant, while Oklahomans say the Longhorns are arrogant.

Adding fuel to the fire is the fact that Oklahoma recruits many of its top players from Texas — a source of annoyance for faithful Longhorn fans. The Red River Rivalry is one of the few games played on a neutral site. The two sides meet in Dallas, halfway between the two schools. Each school gets an equal number of tickets every year. The stadium is divided between Longhorn fans, dressed in burnt orange and white, and Sooner fans, dressed in crimson and cream.

OKLAHOMA VS. TEXAS

Adrian Peterson of the Oklahoma Sooners

HEAD TO HEAD

	OKLAHOMA	TEXAS
Team's First Year	1895	1893
Home Stadium	Gaylord Family Oklahoma Memorial Stadium	Darrell K. Royal-Texas Memorial Stadium
Mascot	Sooner Schooner (Conestoga Wagon)	Bevo (Longhorn Cow)
Colors	Crimson and Cream	Burnt Orange and White

KICKOFF

The first game was played in 1900, before Oklahoma even earned its statehood! Since 1929, the game has been played at the Cotton Bowl in Dallas. It takes place in mid-October during the State Fair of Texas. The selected "home" team rotates every year. Ticket sales for the game are split equally between the two schools, with the stadium divided along the 50-yard line. Since 2000, the second year of the Bob Stoops era, Oklahoma has regained its reputation as a football powerhouse. The Sooners have dominated the Big 12 Conference, winning conference titles in five of the last eight years. In 2000, they won their seventh national championship.

STAR PLAYERS

Oklahoma: Entering his first year at Oklahoma, Adrian Peterson (aka A.D., for "All Day") was widely touted by football experts as the next great Sooner running back. Peterson did not disappoint. In his first year, he set an NCAA freshman rushing record and finished second in the Heisman voting. After three record-setting years at OU, "All Day" was drafted seventh overall by the Minnesota Vikings in the 2007 NFL draft. As a first-year pro, Peterson continued his brilliant running. He broke the NFL's single-game rushing record when he ran for 296 yards against the San Diego Chargers.

Texas: Vince Young was a star quarterback at UT. His height, strength, and athleticism made him a constant threat as both a runner and a passer. During his junior year, he led the Longhorns to their fourth national title (their first since 1970) by winning what was arguably the most exciting championship game of all time. Young led his team to an incredible, final-minute 41–38 come-from-behind victory over the heavily favored USC Trojans. That same year, Young had come in second to USC's Reggie Bush in the Heisman voting. Young was drafted third overall by Tennessee in 2006, where he won the award for NFL Offensive Rookie of the Year.

touted: *promoted or praised energetically; publicized*

Oklahoma and Texas fans fill the Cotton Bowl.

THE SPY GAME

Football is a serious business in the Lone Star State. On Friday nights in autumn, entire towns shut down to watch their local high school teams. Enthusiastic fans are common in football, but Texans take their obsession to a new level. This **account** details two well-known events.

The Red River Rivalry began innocently, but has been fiercely competitive ever since World War II. It has turned into one of the most bitter rivalries in football, peaking in the mid-1970s.

In 1975, Texas coach Darrell Royal accused Oklahoma coach Barry Switzer of unfair recruiting practices. The Sooners had recruited several high-school stars from Texas to attend OU. Though this was not wrong, using Texans to beat UT added to the tension that already existed between the two schools. In 1975, Switzer took and passed a polygraph test. This suggested that he was not guilty of unfair recruiting practices, such as trying to entice top players to join his team by giving them money and other rewards.

A year later in 1976, Royal heard about a "mystery man" who was seen hanging around the Longhorns' practices, which were closed to outsiders. Royal accused Switzer of sending this man to spy on his team. The spy story came out the day before the big game.

Royal offered Switzer $10,000 to take another lie-detector test, but Switzer refused.

The supposed "Spy Game" is remembered as the most bitter of this series. With all of the scandal surrounding the game, the Longhorns badly wanted to beat the Sooners, who had beaten them the previous five years. The game ended in a 6–6 tie. Royal quit coaching after that season. He said he couldn't beat Oklahoma without cheating, and he wouldn't cheat to win.

> **?** How do you feel about cheating in sports? What changes would you suggest to prevent cheating?

Quick Fact
The Red River Rivalry is played with three trophies on the line: 1) the Golden Hat, given to the winner of the game; 2) the Red River Rivalry Trophy, given to the student government of the winning school; 3) the Governor's Trophy, given to the governor of the winning state.

The Expert Says...
"The game has been sold out … since 1946. That's how important it is. … Even though it's sold out, it's still televised nationally."
— Darrell K. Royal, former Texas Longhorn head coach

Take Note
Taking the #4 spot, the Oklahoma-Texas rivalry is definitely one of the most bitter on our list. With past accusations of cheating, this competition is as fierce and angry as any in college football.
- In 2005, the rivalry's name was changed from the Red River Shootout to the Red River Rivalry. Would you have expected this name change to have reduced the bad feelings between these two schools? Why or why not?

3 ALABAMA VS.

Running back Ben Tate of the Auburn Tigers (#44) drags a group of Alabama Crimson Tide defenders on November 24, 2007.

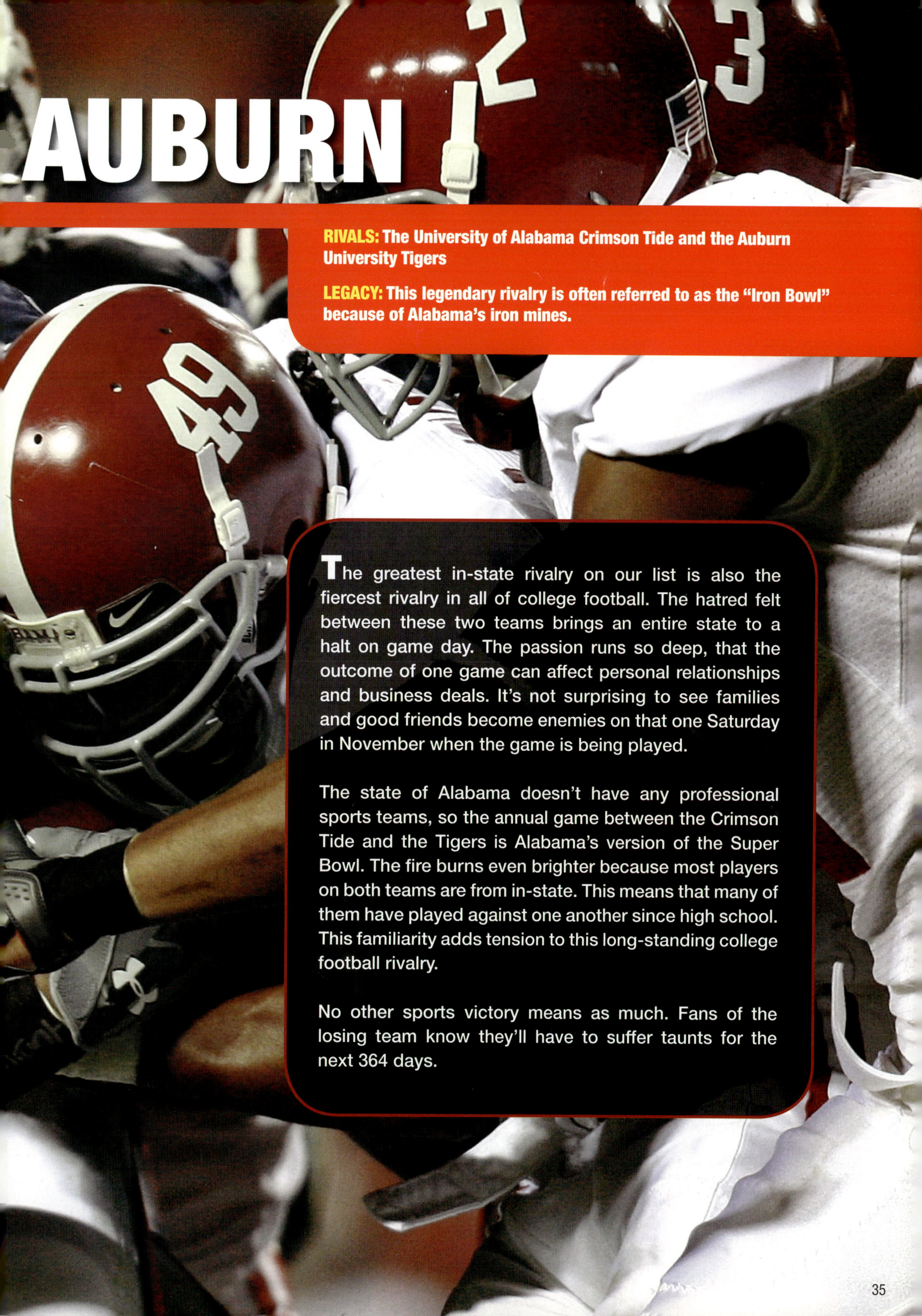

AUBURN

RIVALS: The University of Alabama Crimson Tide and the Auburn University Tigers

LEGACY: This legendary rivalry is often referred to as the "Iron Bowl" because of Alabama's iron mines.

The greatest in-state rivalry on our list is also the fiercest rivalry in all of college football. The hatred felt between these two teams brings an entire state to a halt on game day. The passion runs so deep, that the outcome of one game can affect personal relationships and business deals. It's not surprising to see families and good friends become enemies on that one Saturday in November when the game is being played.

The state of Alabama doesn't have any professional sports teams, so the annual game between the Crimson Tide and the Tigers is Alabama's version of the Super Bowl. The fire burns even brighter because most players on both teams are from in-state. This means that many of them have played against one another since high school. This familiarity adds tension to this long-standing college football rivalry.

No other sports victory means as much. Fans of the losing team know they'll have to suffer taunts for the next 364 days.

ALABAMA VS. AUBURN

HEAD TO HEAD

	ALABAMA	AUBURN
Team's First Year	1892	1892
Home Stadium	Bryant-Denny Stadium	Jordan-Hare Stadium
Mascot	Big Al the Elephant	Aubie the Tiger
Colors	Crimson and White	Burnt Orange and Navy Blue

Bo Jackson of the Auburn Tigers

KICKOFF

The series began in 1893. It stopped between 1908 and 1948 because school administrators could not agree on the amount the players would get for expenses and who would referee the game. But the fans pressured the schools to resume their rivalry. Even the Alabama state legislature wanted the series brought back. In 1948, both schools' presidents agreed that the Iron Bowl should take place again, but at a neutral site in Birmingham, Alabama. Their highly competitive rivalry has since developed into one of the best in college football.

Quick Fact

The winner of the Alabama-Auburn game takes home the James E. Foy, V-ODK Sportsmanship Trophy. This trophy was created by students of the two universities in 1948 as a symbol of good sportsmanship. It was named after Dean James E. Foy, V, who had served at both Auburn and Alabama, and ODK, a leadership society with a presence at both universities.

STAR PLAYERS

Alabama: Joe Namath led his school to a national championship in 1964. As a pro, Namath became famous as the quarterback of the New York Jets who "guaranteed" a win against the favored Baltimore Colts in Super Bowl III. "Broadway Joe" became an instant legend when he delivered on his guarantee by leading the Jets to victory.

Auburn: Bo Jackson was a gifted three-sport athlete. He had an incredible football career that included winning the Heisman Trophy in 1985. His #34 jersey was later retired by Auburn. Jackson went on to great success as a two-sport star in the NFL and Major League Baseball. He was the first athlete to be selected for all-star games in both leagues.

The Expert Says…

" I tell people it's part of our culture. It's a natural thing. The rivalry is woven into everyday life. "

— Ken "The Snake" Stabler, Alabama quarterback (1965–1967)

BATTLE CRIES!

College football rivalries are so intense that they often resemble battles more than sporting events. Fittingly, each side must have its own battle cry to intimidate the enemy. This report explores the origins of this rivalry's famous cries.

ROLL TIDE!

The Alabama football team was originally called the "Crimson White" after the school colors. The "Crimson Tide" nickname came from Hugh Roberts, the sports editor of a Birmingham newspaper in 1907. He used the expression while describing the Alabama-Auburn game, which happened to be the last time the two schools played each other until 1948. Auburn was favored to win the game, but Alabama earned its nickname by holding on for a 6–6 tie. The "Roll Tide" battle cry is a combination of the team's nickname and an Alabama fight song called *Yea Alabama*. The last two verses of the song are, "You're Dixie's football pride, Crimson Tide, Roll Tide, Roll Tide!"

WAR EAGLE!

The "War Eagle" battle cry dates back to 1864. According to legend, an Auburn student who went to fight in the Civil War was wounded in battle but survived and found a baby eagle at his side. He saved the eagle and nursed it back to health. After the war, he took the bird back to Auburn and named it "War Eagle." Years later in 1892, he took the eagle along to an Auburn football game. When Auburn scored its first touchdown, the eagle broke free and soared above the field. Auburn fans started chanting "War Eagle." At the end of the game, the old eagle collapsed and died. To this day, Auburn fans still shout "War Eagle" during games.

? What atmosphere do you think a battle cry would create at a game? How do you think a battle cry would help to motivate a team?

Quick Fact
Alabama's Paul "Bear" Bryant is considered one of the greatest coaches in history. He retired with 323 wins, a record at the time. Bryant was also a football player at Alabama. He proved his toughness by playing against Tennessee with a broken leg.

Take Note
Taking the #3 spot, the Auburn-Alabama showdown is considered by many to be the best in-state rivalry in the country. Alabama followers are especially famous for being fanatical about their team. For many fans, it is a 365-day-a-year passion.
- Why do you think some football fans are so passionate about their teams? Think about something in your life that you are passionate about and explain why it makes you feel this way.

② MICHIGAN VS.

Brian Hartline of the Ohio State University Buckeyes collides with Trent Morgan of the Michigan Wolverines (#14).

OHIO STATE

RIVALS: University of Michigan Wolverines and the Ohio State University Buckeyes

LEGACY: No rivalry has a better combination of history, hostility, and championship talent.

This rivalry has a large following that definitely goes beyond its Midwestern roots. Legends are made and hearts are broken each time the Michigan Wolverines and the Ohio State University (OSU) Buckeyes face each other. When it comes to this rivalry, winning is everything. Every year on the last Saturday before Thanksgiving, more than 100,000 fans pack the Ohio Stadium "Horseshoe" or Michigan's "Big House." Millions more watch the game on television. This rivalry is so big that in 2006, an Ohio election result was put on hold until after the game so that vote counters could watch it on television.

With two of the best college football programs in the country, Michigan and Ohio State feature some of the best athletes playing in some of the most legendary games in college football. Since each school's team routinely ranks among the strongest in the country, the game often has the Big Ten Conference title and the national championship on the line.

Big Ten Conference: *association of 11 institutions, located primarily in the Midwestern United States — Ohio State, Illinois, Michigan, Wisconsin, Penn State, Iowa, Purdue, Michigan State, Indiana, Northwestern, Minnesota*

MICHIGAN VS. OHIO STATE

HEAD TO HEAD

	MICHIGAN	OHIO STATE
Team's First Year	1879	1890
Home Stadium	Michigan Stadium	Ohio Stadium
Mascot	No mascot	Brutus Buckeye
Colors	Maize (Yellow) and Blue	Scarlet and Gray

Drummer in the Ohio State University Marching Band

KICKOFF

Ohio State and Michigan played their first game in 1897. Michigan was victorious, winning 34–0. In fact, Michigan won this match-up for the next 15 years. Since 1918, the game's site has rotated between Columbus, Ohio, and Ann Arbor, Michigan. It has been the last regular-season game on each team's schedule since 1935. It was famed Buckeyes coach Woody Hayes (1969–1978) who really turned this rivalry into a heated war, with his passion and fiery attitude toward all things Michigan.

Quick Fact
There have been streaks in this high-stakes rivalry. Ohio State coach John Cooper was fired in 2001 after defeating Michigan only twice in 13 tries. In 2007, University of Michigan coach Lloyd Carr resigned after losing six of seven games to OSU coach Jim Tressel.

 Do you think coaches are solely responsible for the success of the team? Explain.

STAR PLAYERS

Michigan: Desmond Howard gained national fame in 1991 for striking the "Heisman" stiff-arm pose after returning a punt for a touchdown against Ohio State. He went on to win the Heisman Trophy later that year. As a pro, Howard made another famous punt return for a touchdown in Super Bowl XXXI. The play helped the Green Bay Packers win the game. Howard ended up as the Super Bowl MVP.

Ohio State: Famed Ohio State coach Woody Hayes once said of Archie Griffin: "He's a better young man than he is a football player, and he's the best football player I've ever seen." Griffin is the only two-time winner of the Heisman Trophy — in 1974 and 1975.

punt: kick of the ball by the offensive team to the opponent, sacrificing possession for field position

Michigan Stadium, nicknamed The Big House, can hold more than 110,000 fans.

THE TEN YEAR WAR

THIS REPORT DISCUSSES THE MOST INTENSE DECADE OF THIS RIVALRY.

The Ten Year War was perhaps the best example of this rivalry's excellence. From 1969 to 1978, Michigan and OSU transformed the Big Ten Conference into what some have described as the "Big Two and Little Eight." During this period, Michigan and OSU combined to win the conference title every year, including six years when they shared the honor.

Two famous faces dominated the Ten Year War — Michigan coach Bo Schembechler and OSU coach Woody Hayes. Schembechler had started his coaching career as Hayes's assistant before he was hired to serve as the head coach for rival Michigan after the 1968 season. Though the two men remained good friends, there was an intense rivalry between the teacher and his pupil. In his first season as coach, Schembechler led the Wolverines to a 24–12 upset victory over his former team. OSU had come into the game as the heavy favorite, riding a 22-game winning streak. The two coaches would face each other nine more times before Hayes was eventually fired. Schembechler narrowly led the rivalry 5–4–1.

"If Bo is not a winner, I never saw one and I should know …"
— *Woody Hayes on Bo Schembechler*

"[U]nless you knew him or played for him, it is hard to explain why you liked being around the guy. But you didn't just like it, you loved it. He was simply fascinating."
— *Bo Schembechler on Woody Hayes*

Quick Fact
It is reported that Buckeyes coach Woody Hayes once ran out of gas in Michigan a few miles from the Ohio border. He pushed his car back into Buckeye territory because he refused to spend any money in Michigan!

 How do you think a rivalry between coaches would affect the attitude and morale of their players?

The Expert Says…
On the atmosphere of the Ohio State-Michigan game:

"I remember thinking I was preparing for just another game as a coach. … I wasn't worth a hoot probably the first quarter because I was just in awe of the feeling.

— Jim Tressel, Ohio State football head coach

Take Note
The Ohio State-Michigan rivalry takes the #2 spot on our list. These schools boast two of the best programs in the nation — in 2006, they came into the game undefeated and ranked #1 and #2. The annual showdown has all the makings of a legendary rivalry — passionate coaches, dedicated and loyal fans, fierce competition for national titles, and long-standing hostility.
- Do you think you'd be more motivated to beat your rival if they had an undefeated record? Why or why not?

1 SOUTHERN CALIF

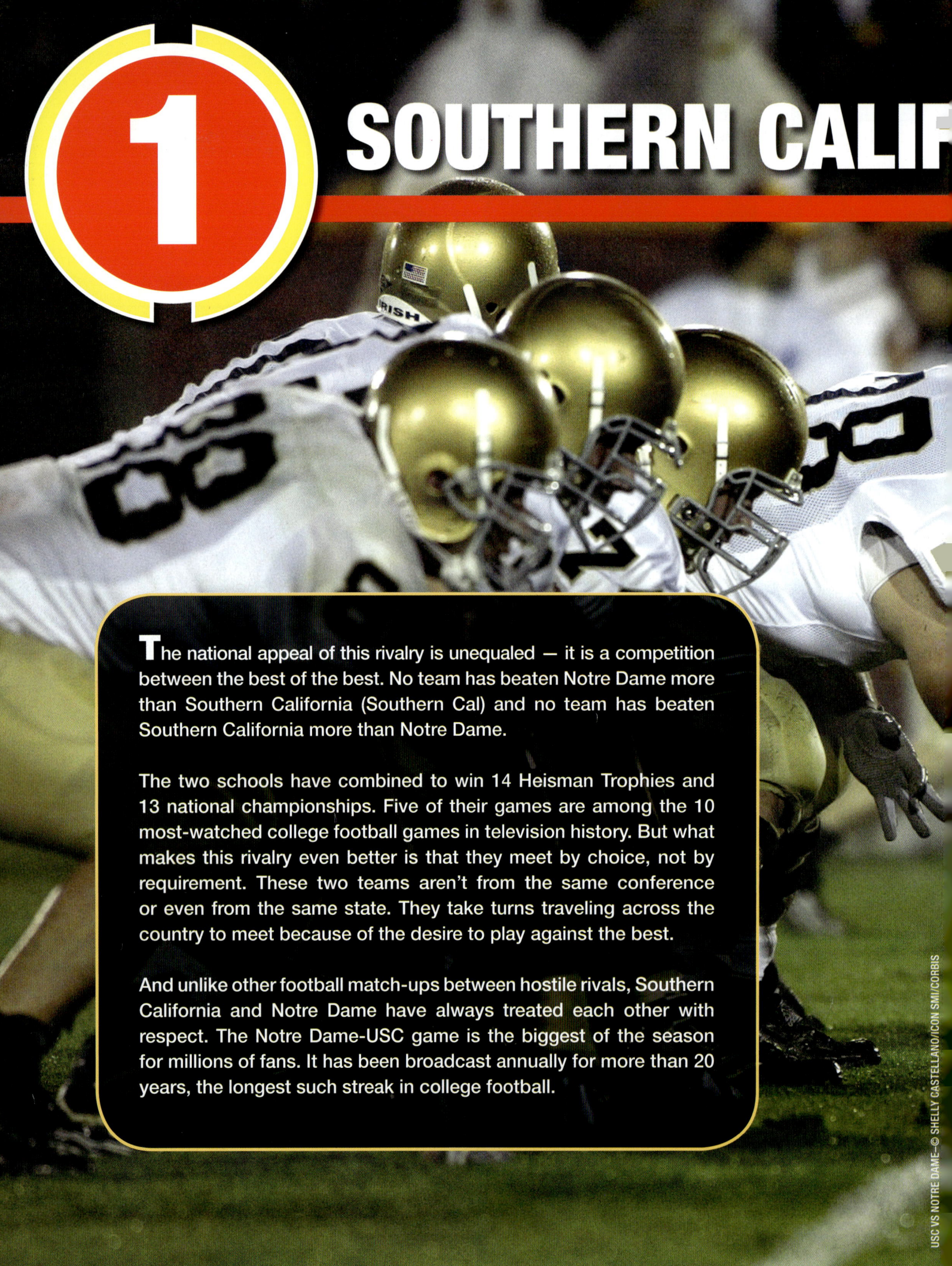

The national appeal of this rivalry is unequaled — it is a competition between the best of the best. No team has beaten Notre Dame more than Southern California (Southern Cal) and no team has beaten Southern California more than Notre Dame.

The two schools have combined to win 14 Heisman Trophies and 13 national championships. Five of their games are among the 10 most-watched college football games in television history. But what makes this rivalry even better is that they meet by choice, not by requirement. These two teams aren't from the same conference or even from the same state. They take turns traveling across the country to meet because of the desire to play against the best.

And unlike other football match-ups between hostile rivals, Southern California and Notre Dame have always treated each other with respect. The Notre Dame-USC game is the biggest of the season for millions of fans. It has been broadcast annually for more than 20 years, the longest such streak in college football.

...ORNIA VS. NOTRE DAME

RIVALS: The University of Southern California Trojans and the University of Notre Dame Fighting Irish

LEGACY: The one and only "national" college football rivalry in the United States.

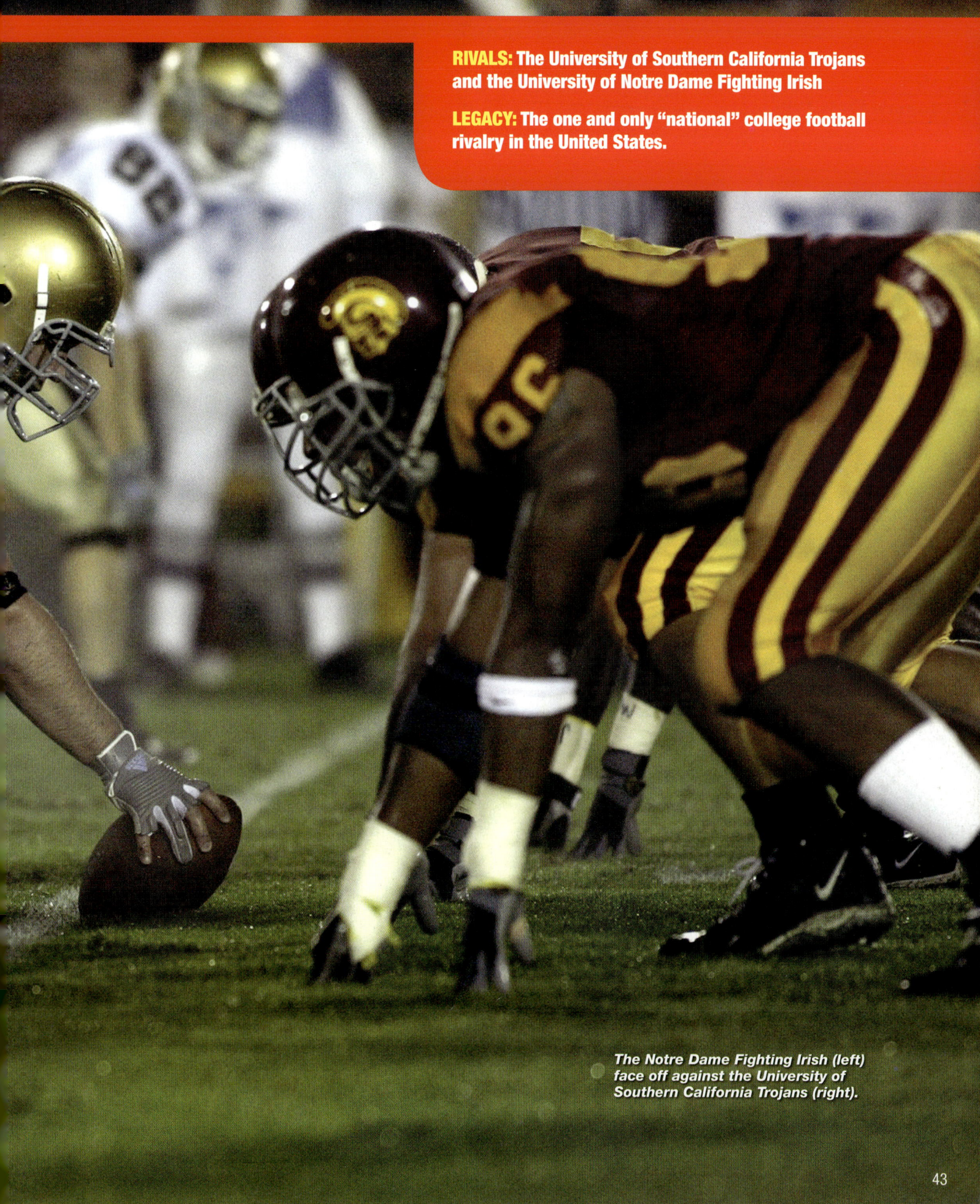

The Notre Dame Fighting Irish (left) face off against the University of Southern California Trojans (right).

Southern California vs. Notre Dame

Head to Head

	NOTRE DAME	SOUTHERN CALIFORNIA
Team's First Year	1887	1888
Home Stadium	Notre Dame Stadium	Los Angeles Memorial Coliseum
Mascot	Leprechaun	Traveler (VII)
Colors	Gold and Blue	Cardinal and Gold

Notre Dame's Paul Hornung

Quick Fact
Southern California tried to recruit legendary coach Knute Rockne from Notre Dame in 1925, a year before the first game was played between the two schools. Rockne led the Fighting Irish from 1918–1930 and set the record for greatest career winning percentage.

Kickoff
In 1925, Southern California was looking for a national rival. As the story goes, the school sent athletic director Gwynn Wilson and his wife to Lincoln, Nebraska, where Notre Dame was playing the University of Nebraska. At first, Notre Dame coach Knute Rockne was not sure about playing the Trojans because of the travel involved. But Mrs. Wilson was able to convince Mrs. Rockne that a trip to sunny California was better than one to snowy Nebraska. Mrs. Rockne spoke to her husband and USC was added to Notre Dame's schedule. The first game was played in 1926 when the Fighting Irish traveled to Los Angeles to play the Trojans. Notre Dame won that first contest with a score of 13–12.

Star Players
Notre Dame: Paul Hornung (aka Golden Boy) is widely considered to be the best player to ever wear the Fighting Irish uniform. He won the Heisman Trophy in 1956 and is the only player to do so while playing for a team with a losing record. Hornung went on to a successful NFL career, which included winning the first ever Super Bowl with the Green Bay Packers.

Southern California: Marcus Allen won the Heisman Trophy in 1981, set an NCAA record for the most career 200-yard rushing games, and had his #33 jersey retired by the Trojans. In the NFL, he made his mark with the Los Angeles Raiders. He received the ultimate honor when he was voted into the Pro Football Hall of Fame in 2003.

The Expert Says...
"It's all of the rich heritage and the history of the match-ups. The classic arenas to play in and the cross-country connection. They have such a great following in the middle of the country and we have the great backing out in the west. It's the great names you remember, from the big-time coaches to all of the special players. Even the colors look good when you play together. You name it, the rivalry has it. It's all just very, very rich and very special."

— Pete Carroll, Southern California head coach (2001–present)

With Notre Dame in Indiana and USC in California, these two schools are very far away from each other. Why do you think distance does not matter for these rivals?

MEMORABLE MOMENTS

Notre Dame and Southern California have had many memorable moments since their first game back in 1926. This report captures four of their unforgettable match-ups.

The Fighting Irish huddle by the sideline during a timeout.

November 21, 1931 | Notre Dame Stadium
USC 16, Notre Dame 14

USC earns its first win over the Irish. The Trojans trail 14–0 at the start of the fourth quarter. After scoring 13 unanswered points, Johnny Baker kicks a 33-yard field goal with one minute left to give USC a 16–14 win. The Fighting Irish's first-ever loss in Notre Dame Stadium is also the team's first loss in 27 games.

November 28, 1964 | The Coliseum
USC 20, Notre Dame 17

First-year Notre Dame coach Ara Parseghian takes the Fighting Irish from unranked at the start of the season to #1 going into this game. The Fighting Irish lead 17–13 with just over a minute left on the clock. Trojan quarterback Craig Fertig throws Rod Sherman a 15-yard touchdown pass to win the game.

November 29, 1986 | The Coliseum
Notre Dame 38, USC 37

This contest was famed Irish coach Lou Holtz's first in the rivalry, and a win would help to reestablish the Notre Dame as a football power. Down 37–20 to start the fourth quarter, Notre Dame rallies with two consecutive touchdowns to narrow the deficit to 37–35. In the final minute, the Irish's Tim Brown returns a punt 56 yards to the Trojan 16-yard line, and John Carney kicks the game-winning field goal.

November 30, 1996 | The Coliseum
USC 27, Notre Dame 20

After 13 seasons without beating their archrival, it looks like USC is headed for another loss as the Fighting Irish take a 20–12 fourth-quarter lead. However, the Irish miss the extra point. USC takes advantage, tying the game with a late touchdown and a two-point conversion. In overtime, the Trojans score a touchdown that earns them a 27–20 victory.

extra point: *after a touchdown, a short field-goal attempt worth one point*

 Notre Dame is the most respected and loved college football team in the country. Despite being a small, private institution, they have a huge national following. How important is the school's rich tradition in contributing to its popular appeal?

Quick Fact
The winner of this game keeps the Jeweled Shillelagh (shil-lay-lah) for a year, which is a Gaelic war club from Ireland made of wood. The shillelagh has emerald-studded shamrocks that stand for Notre Dame wins and ruby-jeweled Trojan heads representing Southern California wins.

Take Note
The Notre Dame-USC rivalry takes the #1 spot on our list. Each school brings a unique character to the game. It's California cool versus Midwestern grit. More than that, this rivalry displays sportsmanship and honor, and boasts legendary coaches and outstanding players.
- What do you like most about this rivalry? Would you rank it #1 and why?

We Thought …

Here are the criteria we used in ranking the 10 most intense football rivalries of all time.

The rivalry:
- Has a long and storied history
- Is filled with rich traditions
- Has passionate and loyal fans
- Has had many memorable games
- Includes great players and coaches
- Has national as well as state appeal
- Involves conference or national titles

What Do You Think?

1. Do you agree with our ranking? If you don't, try ranking these rivalries yourself. Justify your ranking with data from your own research and reasoning. You may refer to our criteria, or you may want to draw up your own list of criteria.

2. Here are three other rivalries that we considered but in the end did not include in our top 10 list: Lehigh vs. Lafayette, Texas vs. Texas A&M, and Grambling vs. Southern University.
   - Find out more about these rivalries. Do you think they should have made our list? Give reasons for your response.
   - Are there other rivalries that you think should have made our list? Explain your choices.

Index

A
Alabama, 29, 34–37
Allen, Marcus, 44

B
Ben Hill Griffin Stadium, 20
Bersin, Alan, 16
Big Ten Conference, 39, 41
Blanchard, Doc, 24
Bowden, Bobby, 28–29
Bryant-Denny Stadium, 36
Bryant, Paul, 37

C
California, 6–9, 42–45
California Memorial Stadium, 6, 8
Carroll, Pete, 44
Civil War: Army vs. Navy, A, 24
Clemson Memorial Stadium, 12
Clemson University Tigers, 10–13
College Football Hall of Fame, 16
Commander-in-Chief's Trophy, 25
Cotton Bowl, 32

D
Darrell K. Royal-Texas Memorial Stadium, 32
Davis, Glen Woodward, 24
Doak Campbell Stadium, 28

E
Elway, John, 8

F
Feinstein, John, 24
Field goal, 9, 29, 45
Florida, 18–21, 26–29
Florida State University Seminoles, 26–29
Frank, Clint, 16

G
Gaylord Family Oklahoma Memorial Stadium, 32
Georgia, 18–21
Golden Hat, 33
Gonzalez, Tony, 8
Governor's Trophy, 33
Grambling State University, 47
Griffin, Archie, 40

H
Harris, Walt, 8
Harvard Stadium, 16–17
Harvard University Crimson, 14–17, 23
Hayes, Woody, 40–41
Heisman, John, 12
Heisman Trophy, 12, 16, 20, 24, 32, 36, 40, 42, 44
Hornung, Paul, 44
Howard, Desmond, 40

I
Iron Bowl, 35–36
Ivy League, 15–16

J
Jackson, Bo, 36
Jacksonville Municipal Stadium, 20
James E. Foy, V-ODK Sportsmanship Trophy, 36
Jeweled Shillelagh, 45

K
Kacyvenski, Isaiah, 16
Kelley, Larry, 16
Kosar, Bernie, 28

L
Lafayette College, 47
Lehigh University, 47
Los Angeles Memorial Coliseum, 44

M
McCormick, Jay, 12
Meyer, Urban, 20
Miami Orange Bowl, 28
Michie Stadium, 24
Michigan, 38–41
Michigan Stadium, 40

N
Namath, Joe, 36
National Collegiate Athletic Association, 8, 32, 44
National Football League, 8, 12, 15–17, 20, 24, 26, 28–29, 32, 36, 44
Navy-Marine Corps Memorial Stadium, 24
Notre Dame Stadium, 44–45

O
Ohio, 38–41
Ohio Stadium, 39–40
Ohio State University Buckeyes, 38–41
Oklahoma, 30–33

P
Perry, William, 12
Peterson, Adrian, 32
Pro Football Hall of Fame, 24, 44

Q
Quarterback, 8, 12–13, 20–21, 24, 28–29, 32, 36, 45

R
Red River Rivalry, 31, 33
Red River Rivalry Trophy, 33
Rockne, Knute, 44
Rogers, George, 12
Royal, Darrell K, 33
Running back, 12, 21, 32, 34

S
Sanders, Deion, 28
Sanford Stadium, 20
Schembechler, Bo, 41
South Carolina, 10–13
Southeastern Conference, 19
Southern University, 47
Spurrier, Steve, 20
Stabler, Ken, 36
Stanford Axe, 8
Stanford Stadium, 8
Stanford University Cardinal, 6–9
Staubach, Roger, 24
Sugar Bowl, 21
Super Bowl, 8, 24, 35–36, 40, 44
Switzer, Barry, 33

T
Tackler, 16, 21
Texas, 30–33, 47
Texas A&M University, 47
Tressel, Jim, 40–41

U
United States Military Academy Black Knights, 22–25
United States Naval Academy Midshipmen, 22–25
University of Alabama Crimson Tide, 34–37
University of California, Berkeley Golden Bears 6–9
University of Florida Gators, 18–21
University of Georgia Bulldogs, 18–21
University of Miami Hurricanes, 26–29
University of Michigan Wolverines, 38–41
University of Notre Dame Fighting Irish, 42–45
University of Oklahoma Sooners, 30–33
University of South Carolina Gamecocks, 10–13
University of Southern California Trojans, 42–45
University of Texas at Austin, 47
University of Texas Longhorns, 30–33

W
Walker, Herschel, 20–21

Y
Yale Bowl, 16
Yale University Bulldogs, 14–17, 23
Young, Vincent, 32